chasers of the light

poems from the typewriter series

-Tyler Knott Gregson-

追逐光的男人和他的打字機

泰勒·諾特·葛瑞格森

SLY

心思

序言

序言，就我的理解，應該要從頭說起。從故事的頭，從旅程的頭，從妳叨絮自己是如何走到今日、那些大話傳奇的頭。

　　這故事原本可以從好幾個不同的地方起頭——從我十二歲寫下第一首詩的那一天，或者從我開始有「每日一詩」寫作習慣的那一天。但是，我打算從我在蒙大拿州海勒拿（Helena, Montana）的一間骨董店裡買下我第一台打字機說起。

　　我記得這台打字機聞起來的味道，就像灰塵和乾掉的墨漬。我記得那些打字鍵，還有我頭一回試打的時候它們是如何卡住的。我記得機器上褪色的「雷明頓（Remington）」字樣。而我記得最清楚的，是打字機裡的色帶還留有油墨，足夠讓我打完「打字機系列」的第一首詩，也是這本書裡的第一首詩。我從一本用兩塊錢買來的舊書上撕下一頁，就這麼站在門邊，在店裡打下了這首詩。我打字的時候不作斟酌，毫無計畫，也沒有辦法做任何修改。

　　我愛上了這種感覺。

我愛這種迫切感，使用打字機時無法修改、編輯、與調整內容的那種無能為力，和不被中斷的思緒。我愛這些紙頁映照出我的內心的方式：沒有篩選、沒有完美、只有坦率真誠。在數位化的世界裡，這就好像是一股擁抱住類比文字的清新空氣。

多年以來，身為一名攝影師與作家，我已經找到許多以外顯的方式表達內在事物的方法。而在這些詩中，我更了解到它們原來都依循著一條共同的脈絡。不論這些詩是在一張隨手撿來的紙條上、在被塗黑的書頁上、或者是伴隨我拍攝的照片出現，它們都試著要做到兩件事：

將巨大的事物、偉岸的姿態、澎湃的情感化為細小的微光、碎片。

抓住微小的片刻、溜走的時間、與稍縱即逝的光陰，將它們放大。

平凡中見奇蹟，質樸造就史詩。

我曾經寫道，我是一個記憶的守護者，我設下了捕捉時間的陷阱；我寫我偷了流逝的光陰，我是竊取被深埋的恐懼的賊。我寫我是追逐光的人。經過了這段時間的書寫，拍攝了這麼多照片，我愈發感受到這幾句話的真切。在我所寫所言當中，我試著要去追逐身邊令我忍不住想探視的光芒。這本書，最簡單的說法，就是一本記錄我追尋過程的行跡地圖。信手取來的紙張、簡單的字句，就這麼一路悄然地溜進我的生活裡。光一直都在，而我也不會停下追逐的腳步。

What if all we have ever wanted
        isn't hiding in some
secret and faraway dream
        but inside of us now
    as we breathe one another
and find home in the way
    our arms always seem to fit
perfectly around the spaces
        between us?
What if we are the answer
        and love was the question?
What if all this time
it was us you were supposed
            to find?
I am filled with wonderings
    questions and doubt
    but of one thing I am certain:
it will always be you
        that gives flight to the
    butterflies inside me,
    calm to the sea I have become
and hope to the darkness
        all around us.
    It is you and it has always
been you...
you.
        You that soothes and excites
    and spreads joy like rainfall
on the already damp earth;
You that pulled me from the longest
sleep and kissed my tired eyelids
            awake.
    If life is a question mark,
        then you, my love,
    are the proud and bold period
that is typed with certainty.

會不會我們始終追求的一切
從來不是藏在那些
祕密且遙遠的夢境，而是
正當我們呼吸、
正當
我們因為雙臂在我們之間似乎總是自在、
感到心有所屬時，
它就存在我們內在？
會不會
我們才是「愛」這個問題的答案？
會不會一直以來
妳該覓得的就是我們？
我滿是納悶、
疑惑與不解
但有件事我毫無疑問：
是妳
讓我心中的蝴蝶
翩翩飛翔，
平靜了我的海洋
為我們四周的黑暗帶來希望。
是妳，一直都是妳⋯⋯
妳。
妳撫慰、妳振奮
妳散播歡樂如遍撒甘霖
在這沉頹已久的大地
妳引我走出長眠
輕吻我睏倦的雙眼
將我喚醒。
倘若人生是個問號，
那麼妳，吾愛
妳就是那帶著肯定「打」下的
昂然而明白的句號。

和我去走趟老鐵軌吧,一聽到聲音我們就跑。把我們的耳朵貼在溫熱的金屬上,猜猜看隆隆地車聲還有多久會來到我們眼前,撼動我們的心靈。追吧,把手伸長、跳進車廂裡,隨它載我們到哪兒去。有時候我們想飛奔回家,有時候我們急著離開;至於什麼時候、會怎麼做,就要看我們人到時候在哪裡了,很棒是不是?當妳發現自己兩手空空,妳便歸心似箭;倘若妳掌心滿滿,妳會更渴望去闖蕩天下。

```
I Love You,
in ways
you've never been
loved,
for reasons you've never been
told,
for longer than you think you
deserved
and with more
than you will ever know existed
inside
me.
```

我愛妳，
用一種妳從未被愛過的方式、
妳從未被告知過的理由；
比起妳以為妳應得的時間更久
也比起妳能想像的更多愛
就在我內心深處。

I think your applause died out,
hands red, tired, and stained
with the hue of once excited blood.
I think you thought I was magic.
Did my curtain lift when I forgot
to take my bow?
I think you thought you saw mirrors
hiding in the fog and light.
Backstage and alone
I will slide off the cape,
set down the hat,
and bow to the empty seat
I thought you were filling.
I think you thought I was magic.

我想妳掌聲漸息，
妳的手紅了、累了，
還透著一時激昂的血色。
我想妳以為我有種魔力。
我忘了鞠躬的時候，布幕是否升起？
我想妳以為妳看見了藏在霧與光中的那面鏡。
我在後台獨自一人時，
會卸掉斗篷，脫下帽子，
想像那空坐位上有妳致意。
我想妳以為我有種魔力。

for 至於

us 我們

THERE is only one wish 唯一的心願

to 是

be 成為

adventurous pioneers 大膽的拓荒者

and 並且

find ourselves
at the end.

最終
找回本心。

Ever
Walk in
Hope,
even
though
there be
no Goal
to Reach

I will miss you
always,
even in the moments
when you are right
beside me.
Time apart has planted
longing inside me
and I do not think
it is a weed
that will ever stop
growing.
It will always live there,
but my god
it grows the most
spectacular
flowers.

我會一直惦著妳，
就算此時此刻
妳正陪伴在
我的身邊。
別離在我心裡
種下了思念
我不認為那是雜草
而某天它會
停止生長蔓延。
它就住在那兒，
但老天，
它綻放了
最燦爛的
花顏。

The words aren't falling
out of my mouth
in the same ways
anymore.
Once they felt like water,
they leaked
and rose
and baptized me new,
halo fresh without the glow.
They explode now,
confetti in a slight breeze
and I am racing around
to pick up the pieces.

話從我口中
說出的方式
已經不同於
以往。
曾經它們如水，
流洩、
滿溢、浸潤我
以氾濫的新鮮光暈，
不帶激情。
現在它們爆炸了，
碎成微風中的五彩斑斕
我只管四處追逐
撿拾那散落的的隻字片語。

Find my hand
in the darkness
and if we
cannot find
the light,
we
will always
make our
own.

在黑暗中
我找尋我的手
如果我們
覓不得
燈火，
我們總會
自己創造
光明。

我依舊在那裡，靜靜地等待著。在水下，在山巔。我依舊在那裡，靜靜地盼望著。在染透樹葉的顏色中，在迎來黑夜的深藍中。我依舊在那裡，等著妳回來。

Peel back my skin and it won't be bones you will find.
Hiding under the muscles the tissues the scars
and the freckles are decaying timbers washed ashore.
I am a sinking ship made of unsinkable parts.
I am an old boat, built without a rudder,
a tattered sheet for a sail.
Can you see what I've been trying to show you,
that I go where the breeze decides to carry me
and you, my love, are a hurricane.

I am made from the creaking beams and rusted nails
of a lonely vessel on a lonely sea.
I am covered and coated, dusted with old salt water
and the frail residue of moonlight.
The oars and the compass, the anchor and the wheel,
have long since abandoned me.
Can you hear what I've longed to tell you,
that I go where the waves wish to deliver me
and you, my love, are the tide.

Press your ear to my chest and listen,
where a heartbeat should sing you will hear
the melancholy songs of tired whales.
The unsettled sigh and explosion of breath
as they find the surface once again.
Can you taste the salt on my lips?
Can you listen to the words I've been aching to say,
that I go where the lights pull me
and you, my love, are the stars.

Stare through the portholes of my eyes
across the grey blue and green they float upon.
Hold tight to the timbers hiding under this flesh
and fill the empty sail with your grace.
I am the fragments of a shattered ship
filled with ancient songs sung by ancient souls.
Can you feel me falling into you as you leak into me,
that I am a sinking ship made from sinking parts
and you, my love, are the sea.

剝開我的皮膚，妳看到的不會是骨頭。
藏在肌肉、組織、傷疤、和雀斑底下的，是被沖上岸的朽木。
我是一艘用不沉的零件打造的沉船。
我是一艘無舵的老船，連一張可以揚起的破帆也沒有。
妳是否看見我一直想讓妳看的──
我會任憑微風將我帶向天涯，而妳，我的愛，妳是颶風。

我是危桁與鏽釘
來自寂寞海上的一葉孤舟
陳年鹹水與微弱、細碎的月光灑了我一身
我被掩藏覆蓋。
那些槳、羅盤、錨、和舵輪，早已把我拋棄。
妳能否聽見我一直渴望告訴妳的──
我會任憑波濤將我送往海角，而妳，我的愛，妳是浪潮。

將妳的耳朵緊貼我胸口聆聽，
妳會聽見我的心跳唱出了疲憊鯨魚的哀歌。
洶湧的嘆息與奮力的呼吸，
當牠們再次尋得水面之時。
妳能否輕嚐我唇上的鹽粒？
妳能否讓我傾訴我一直想說的那些話語，
那就是我會任憑光將我牽引，
而妳，我的愛，妳是星星。

凝視的目光看穿了灰藍與綠，
直透我漂浮雙眼的舷窗。
抓緊藏在我肉身下的船梁，
用妳的慈悲裝滿這空蕩蕩的孤船。
我是那破船的殘軀，
承載著祖靈吟唱的古調。
妳能否感覺當妳將我滲透，我也正向妳陷落──
我是一艘用沉沒的零件打造的沉船，
而妳，我的愛，妳是大海。

Come here
and take off your clothes
and with them
every single worry
you have ever carried.
My fingertips on your back
will be the very last thing
you will feel
before sleeping
and the sound of my smile
will be the alarm clock
to your morning ears.
Come here
and take off your clothes
and with them
the weight of every yesterday
that snuck atop your shoulders
and declared them home.
My whispers will be the soundtrack
to your secret dreams
and my hand
the anchor to the life
you will open your eyes to.
Come here
and take off your clothes.

過來吧

褪下妳的衣

和妳懷抱的所有憂思

一起褪下。

我的指尖

會在妳背上輕撫

直到妳

酣然入眠；

我的笑聲會做妳的鬧鐘，

清晨時在妳的耳邊

喚妳。

過來吧

褪下妳的衫

和著昨日種種

悄悄地溜上妳肩頭

賴著再也不走的重量

一起褪下。

我的低語

會為妳的私密夢境配樂

而我的手

會做安定妳生活的錨

讓妳盡情去探索世界。

過來吧

褪下妳的衣衫。

I   was amazed,

我   又驚又喜，

妳的唇   找到了

your lips   found

me 我   your pulse

妳的脈搏

your eyes

妳的眼

leave you

留妳

for 在我

me 身邊

噢我的心，你就這樣逃走，
在別人的胸膛裡溫柔地跳動。
若我們不曾被毫無保留地愛過，是否還算活著？
若我們曾經被無比深刻地愛過，是否還會死去？
沒了氣息後我們得到的愛未曾稍歇，
是不是，永恆就存在其中？

Find the positivity. Find the grace. Find it
and hold it and cling to it like it is your
lifeline and only breath of air before
everything sinks. Find the silver linings.
Hold them in your lungs and search for them in
the bubbles and rubble of all that pours down
around you. Find the bright spot in the dark
clouds, listen for the sounds of the birds when
the winds pick up and tear down the house around
you. It is there, shhh, it is there, it is always
there and it is waiting for you to reach out
with both hands, bloody and shaking, and hold
tight to it like it is the last thing you will
ever learn how to let go. Find the glory, the glory
through the ache, and understand that it is what
we can endure that defines who we become. That
it has never been about the punches we can throw,
but the punches we can absorb and still stand
up from. It is the standing up, it has always
been the standing up and the refusal to lie still
and quiet as the numbers count towards ten and
the knockout becomes complete.

Rise my soul, rise through the flame and the ash,
rise through the waters that fill the spaces
under your arms as they crawl toward your throat.
Rise and find the grace, for it is all around you.

Find it. Find the grace.

發現正向的意義；發現恩典。去發現，然後緊緊抓住不放，就當它是一切沉沒前唯一的救命索、唯一的一口空氣。發現一絲希望。往傾瀉在你身上的泡沫和瓦礫裡找尋，讓它們充盈你的心胸。發現烏雲裡的亮點，在狂風摧殘你的屋舍時聆聽鳥兒的鳴唱。在那兒，噓，就在那兒，它一直都在，等著你伸出雙手，血淋淋、顫巍巍的雙手；將它緊緊抓住，彷彿你從來不曾懂得如何放手。發現榮耀，疼痛裡透著的榮耀，你知道我們所能忍受的，終將定義我們成為什麼樣的人。關鍵從來不在我們能揮出什麼拳頭，而在我們能承受住重擊，並且站得抬頭挺胸。抬頭挺胸，要的就是這抬頭挺胸、在讀秒時刻也絕不讓自己靜靜躺在地上任憑擊倒或成定局的反骨。

讓我的靈魂浮現吧，從火燄與灰燼裡浮現，從你臂膀下，不斷沿著喉嚨漫溢的大水中浮現。讓恩典浮現，發現恩典；它正一直圍繞在你身邊。

去發現，發現恩典。

Amazing
how manageable
life
can feel
with only
one blanket
and the right
two arms.

沒想到
只要
一條毛毯
和健全的雙臂
就能讓人感到
生活
竟然
在掌握之間。

When my arms
wrap around you
can you feel
my fingers
clinging
to the fabric
of your clothes?
"You hug me
like I might blow
away,"
you whispered,
but all the fabric
wrapped in all my
fingers was not to
keep you here,
but to go with you
when you did.

當我的雙臂
團團圈住妳的時候
妳是否感覺到
我的手指
也緊抓住
妳的衣衫
不放？
「你這樣抱我
好像我會被
吹散似的，」
妳低聲說道。
但我手指
緊抓過的衣衫
從來沒能
留妳在我身邊，
相反地總是
隨著妳離開了。

靜默
with no word

spoken we
無言 我們

lay down 躺著 and 也

賠了
made

amends for a lack of
罪 因為 少了

us 我們

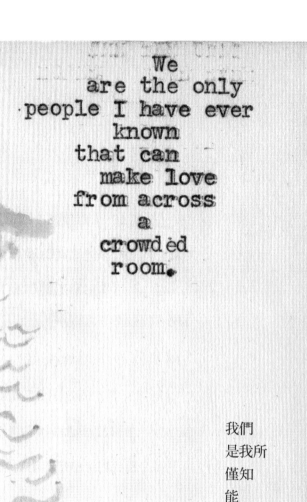

We
are the only
people I have ever
known
that can
make love
from across
a
crowded
room.

我們
是我所
僅知
能
隔著
一整個
擁擠的
房間
做愛
的人。

We are made of passion. We are
made of the half-lid glance out
of the eyes glazed over. We are
the long sigh when the weight of
one rests on the chest of the other
after the exhaustion of intimacy
collapses arms. We are the foreheads
slowly touching and the shaking
arms cradling and the quiet reach
of a strong hand to bring lips
closer and kisses deeper and
whispers sweeter. We are the
emotion that has never fit inside
either of us and never will.
We are the crumpled sheets and
pillows fallen to the floor.
The hair disheveled and the out-
paced breath and the quivering
skin that follows.
We are the passion.

我們是激情組成的。是微睜的迷濛雙眼。是熾情狂愛過後癱軟在彼此胸膛上發出的長長嘆息。我們是緩緩輕觸的前額，環抱、搖擺著的雙臂，是靜靜地伸出讓雙唇更靠近、讓吻更深、讓低語更醉人的那隻有力的手。我們是從來不曾、未來也不會安住在彼此心裡的情感。我們是弄皺的床單與散落一地的枕頭。是凌亂的頭髮，急促的呼吸，與隨之而來的微顫的皮膚。

我們是激情的化身。

我不知道我可是屋頂？破舊殘缺得多過完整；而妳是光，閃耀著、美麗了我的罅隙……或，我是光，妳是怕丟掉木瓦和鐵釘的屋頂，沉浸在我的溫暖裡，直到妳忘卻破碎受傷。我不知道。也不知，我究竟會不會知道。

You have never
had to steal
my breath
or take it away,
somehow
you have always
managed to convince me
to hand it over
freely.

妳從不需要
竊取
我的呼吸
或把它帶走，
妳總是
有辦法說服我
乖乖地
將它送上。

Sometimes you look up and there just seems
to be so many more stars than ever before.
More. They burn brighter and they shine
longer and they never vanish into your
periphery when you turn your head. It's as if
they come out for us and to remind us that
their light took so longto come to us, that
if we never had the patience to wait, we
never would have seen them here, tonight,
like this.

That as much as it hurts, sometimes it's
all you can do, wait, endure and keep
shining, knowing that eventually, your light
will reach where it is supposed to reach
and shine for who it is supposed to shine
for.

It is never easy, but it is always worth it.

有時候，我們抬頭仰望，會覺得天上的星星前所未有的
多。多不勝數。光芒更亮、閃耀的時間更長，不論怎麼轉
頭，星星們都不會從周圍消失。彷彿是為我們而來到眼前
的「光」在訴說，它花了好長的時間，要是沒有耐心等待，
就沒有辦法看到，如同今晚，在此時此刻。

雖然痛苦，但有時候我們能做的，只是等待、忍耐、並且
不斷地發光發亮，我們知道終究有一天，我們的光會到達
該去的地方，只為，該看見的人而閃耀。

這從來就不容易，但絕對是值得的。

我們必須 we must
live
活在

in 寧靜
stillness 之中。

Maybe if I
were instead
a baby bird,
you wouldn't always
have to come up
with excuses
for holding me,
soft and tender
in your hands.
Maybe if I
were instead
a baby bird,
I wouldn't always
have to come up
with excuses
for not flying away
from here.

或許，若我是隻小雛鳥，
妳就不必總是得找出各種理由
小心翼翼地捧我在妳手心。
或許，若我是隻小雛鳥，
我就不必總是得找出各種理由
停留在妳身邊不肯飛去。

She rolled over,
buried half her face
in her pillow,
and smiled
slightly.
It was then,
the overwhelming
realization
washed over me,
that there is
so much more
to life
than simply
surviving it.

她翻過身，
臉龐半埋
枕頭裡，
淺淺地
一笑。
這一刻，
排山倒海的領悟
將我澆灌，
原來生命
除了
活下去之外，
還有如此
豐富
美好。

I love
you.
Tell me the words
you need to hear
and I
will say them.
Over and over and over
until the echo sings
like whispered hymns
in the broken rubble
where churches
once stood.

我愛
妳。
告訴我
妳想聽什麼
我就
說什麼。
我會一再、一再、一再地說著
成了回聲、輕唱，
如同讚美詩
在曾經矗立的教堂
破瓦殘礫中
飄蕩。

妳可願意跟我往那條泥濘的老路走去，教自己迷失在山裡？妳可願意把地圖撕碎，在繽飛的紙片中翩翩起舞？且與我追逐地平線，一路找回我們自己。這些流浪的步履正等著妳同行。

What good
is a half-lit
life?
You
can burn me
to ashes
as long as I know
we lived a life
alight.

半明不暗
的日子
有什麼好？
妳
儘管燃燒我
成灰燼
我只知
我們曾經活得
這樣燦爛。

JE T'AIME

Your lips come to rest
gently atop mine
and I feel the words
I Love You
simmering beneath their surface.
You speak them
and touching as they are,
my lips like marionettes
are moved in time
with each syllable.
Your declaration
becomes my proclamation
without me ever
having uttered
a sound.

我愛妳

妳的唇輕輕地
停在我的唇上
我感覺到
「我」「愛」「妳」這幾個字
在唇下微微顫著。
妳說了
動人的三個字，
我的唇
如同牽線人偶般
隨著每個音節而動作。
妳的聲明
成為我
無須開口
安靜的
宣言。

我們絕對

we must

不要

never **while**

forget 忘記，

就算 我們在

we sit wavering

of 勇氣面前

courage,

遲疑，

to 也要

have 懷抱　　**hope** 希望。

Sometimes
the only way
to catch
your breath
is to
lose it
completely.

有時候
要抓住
妳的呼吸
唯一的方法
就是
完全地
失去。

I want to hear your breath,
the slow and steady rhythm
and rise and fall
and fall and rise
as it rocks me to sleep
and I want to see your eyes
open one at a time
to the brightness
of new mornings.
I want to know what your skin
feels like after three days
of traveling and no bother
of a shower because what
we see is more and worth
more than how we feel.
I want to hold your hand
and feel the squeeze when you
are absolutely terrified.
I want to see you smile
when you are worn out from
making love to me and I want
to carry your limp arms
into the shower to let
the warmth soothe us
back to life.

我想聽見妳的呼吸，
緩慢而平穩的節奏
起而伏
伏而起
帶我進入夢鄉。
我想看見妳的雙眼
逐一睜開，
迎向新晨的
燦光。
我想知道妳的肌膚
在旅行三日後是什麼樣的觸感，
不必先沖澡了，
因為我們看到的比我們感受到的
要來得更多也更重要。
我想要牽住妳的手
感受妳驚慌害怕時的
緊緊一握。
我想看到
妳因為與我做愛而虛脫無力時
露出的微笑。
然後我想要
扶著妳癱軟的雙臂走進浴室
讓水流的溫暖撫過我們
帶我們重回人間。

如果光明漸漸消退
沒入黑夜，
讓振翅的聲音，
唱出妳的歸期。
如果黑夜會弄髒
妳的翅膀，
就循著我的低語，
帶妳遠離。

XXVI

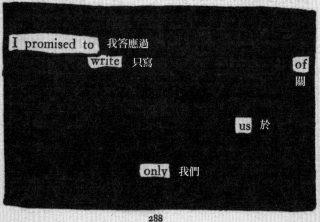

I promised to 我答應過
write 只寫
of 關
us 於
only 我們

What should I say
when I want to kiss
the side of your neck
and leave it at that?
When I want to feel the heat
of my own breath bounce back
and warm my lips after I
strategically place them
on my favorite pieces
of your skin.
I want to leave goosebumps
everywhere I have not yet
kissed and spend the night
trying to read them
like Braille.

當我想親吻
妳的頸側
就這樣
要怎麼說呢？
我想感覺我呼氣
回彈的熱度
溫暖我的唇
我意猶未盡
圖謀妳的肌膚
我最愛的地方。
教雞皮疙瘩留在
每一吋我還沒親吻的地方
然後用整晚的時間
如觸摸點字書般
細細讀它。

Now I Lay Me Down to Sleep . . .

```
Be gentle,
always delicate
with every soul
you meet,
for every single morning
you wake up,
there is someone
Wishing,
silently
and secretly,
that they
had not.
```

此刻我躺下準備入眠……

溫柔地，
始終用心對待
與妳相遇的靈魂，
因為
在妳起身的
每日早晨，
總有人
悄悄地
偷偷地
盼著，
盼自己仍在睡夢中
浮沉。

I am haunted
by the things I miss
and the times my name
doesn't fill your mouth.

I need a word
for the way that feels,
for all the combinations
of all the letters
dont seem to say it
properly.

我心煩意亂
怕錯過了美好
怕妳不再喊著
我的名字。

我要找一個字
表達我的感受，
是遍尋世上所有的字
都難以
說得貼切的
感受。

I count the syllables
of your laughter
and wait
for the line breaks
of your long deep breaths.
I may be a writer
but you are a poem
and you spill out
like ink
onto the paper
of our days.

我數著妳
笑聲的音節
等著為妳
勻長而深沉的呼吸
換行。
我是個作家
而妳卻是首詩
如墨般
潑灑在
寫著我們歲月的
紙張上。

Maybe I
was born
with you
inside me.
Maybe I
have always
carried you
with me.
Maybe you
are all
the wild
in me.

或許
我出生時
妳就在
我身體裡。
或許
我總是
帶著妳
形影不離。
或許
妳是我
內在狂野的
一切。

Promise me
you will not spend
so much time
treading water
and trying to keep your
head above the waves
that you forget,
truly forget,
how much you have always
loved
to swim.

答應我
妳不會把時間
都用來
奮力踩水
好讓妳的頭
保持在水面上，
妳是忘了，
完完全全地忘了，
自己曾經多麼地
熱愛
游泳。

8愛上他修長的身形與高挺的鼻子。他總是站得抬頭挺胸，從不彎腰駝背，勇於承擔領導眾人的責任，讓她傾慕不已。1迷戀於她的曲線，與她欣然接受自己天生外型的勇氣。他愛她不顧眾人眼光，總是微笑著。他們一起離開了海勒拿山丘（Helena Downs），在其他人早已安身立命之時，他們作出了大膽的決定。他們都聽過上回某人離開的八卦，是傳奇的10，他也放手一搏，但終究狼狽歸來，不光變了樣子，也不復存在往日光彩。然而他們還是離開了。從此再沒人見過1和8的身影。

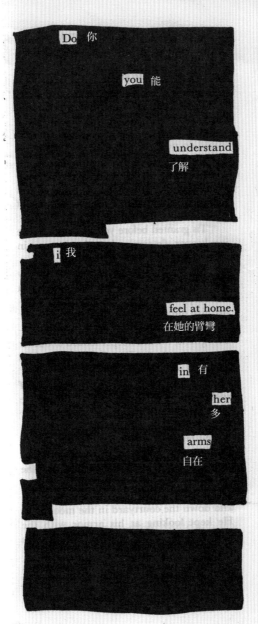

Do 你

you 能

understand
了解

i 我

feel at home.
在她的臂彎

in 有

her
多

arms
自在

91

```
Should I,
this I
nearly asleep
before you,
take pride
in the fact
that I,
this I,
quiet hands
and waiting lips,
know you,
this you
decorating the bed
with your skin,
and all the spots
that make you
shiver?
```

我、
在妳面前
幾乎動彈不得
的我,
是否該以此
為榮?——
我、
雙手安安份份
而雙唇蠢蠢欲動
的我,
是如此地熟悉妳、
裸裎的肌膚
彷若床上美景的妳,
與令妳
顫抖的
每一處。

多仰望，少低頭。多看，少說。多
懷抱希望，少擔心懼怕。多信任，
少苛求。多贊同，少否定。多斷然
拒絕，少不置可否。多歡笑，少哭
泣。多一些愛，少一些憎恨。思
索。愈加思索，愈能心領神會。

I want kisses without question marks
and if at some point one lingers
I want the passion we share
to make those marks stand at attention,
straighten their backs
and transform themselves back
into the exclamation marks
that used to and always should
lock themselves to our lips.

我要不帶問號的吻
偶爾有問號徘徊逗留
我就要用我們濃烈的感情
讓它們一個個立正站好，
背脊挺直，
把它們變成
本該一直停留在
我們唇上的
驚嘆號。

Can't you see
from where you
sit
that I have scars
to kiss?
Can't you hear
from where you
rest
that I just may be
crazy?
Can't you feel
from where you
sleep
that it's always
You
that I
miss?

妳在那兒
坐著，
難道看不見
我的傷痕
正等待著妳的
親吻？
妳在那兒
歇息著，
難道聽不見
我就要
陷入瘋狂了？
妳在那兒
睡著，
難道感覺不到
讓我
朝思暮想的
全都是
妳？

if you are quiet 若妳沉默不語

I 我

wait until
會靜待

you 妳

Tell me 告訴我

告訴我 Tell me what you

dream 妳的

of 夢境

I do not need the photos,
and the taste of envelope glue
does not need to dance atop my tongue.
I will never need the unsaid words,
or the ink stains from unwritten letters,
or the bits of clothing left loose,
crumpled and soundless
beneath the bottom of the sheets.
I will keep you here, always here,
where the nameless things sleep sound.
I will keep you here, hidden here,
as a familiar sensation on the tips
of long untouched fingers,
the abandoned hallways begging
for a ghost, and the smell I cannot place
but has never forgotten me.

我不需要照片，
信封黏膠的滋味不必在我舌尖上跳舞。
未曾說出口的話語，
還沒寫的信與墨漬，
或零亂而安靜地散落在床單下的衣衫，
這些我都不需要。
我會留妳在這裡，一直在這裡，
在這個萬物酣睡的地方。
我會留妳在這裡，藏妳在這裡，
妳就像是久未被碰觸的指尖
曾有的熟悉感受，
荒廢的門廊渴求魅影到來，
還有我無以名之卻始終如影隨形的氣味。

一個彈殼與初綻的花朵。
拾起毀滅過後的餘燼，賦予它新意；
殘害生靈的子彈，也能化為滋養生命的花器。

You should know this,
that I love you
that I have always
loved you
and nothing,
no force in this
universe,
can stop me
from loving you
still.

妳該是清楚的，
我愛妳，
我自始至終
都愛著妳，
在這世界上，
沒有任何事物、
任何力量，
能阻止我
一往情深地
愛妳。

F - B66r0

When we
are we
and a closet
we share,
I
will hang my clothes
in the opposite direction
as yours,
because after a wait
like this,
I think even they
deserve to always
be walking
directly towards
each other.

當我們
共同擁有
一個衣櫥,
我會
將我的衣物掛在
妳的另一邊,
經過如此
漫長的等待,
我想就連它們也都
值得能夠隨時
筆直而
毫無懸念地
走向對方的懷抱。

189

I 我　　　am 是

desolate

a 名　　　孤獨的

wanderer
浪人

with 帶著

feet 步履　　worn out
�

一路伴我

all this while I

went 獨行　　alone
踽踽

Prayer
祈禱

If I died tonight
I think I
would like to come back
as your morning
coffee.
Just as strong
and just
as necessary.

-Tyler Knott Gregson-

若我今晚死去
我想我會回到妳身邊
化作一杯早晨的咖啡。
如此濃烈
又如此不可或缺。

—泰勒‧諾特‧葛瑞格森—

My arms aren't quite long enough
to wrap all around myself,
and I have discovered
that interlocked fingers
on the small part of the spine
make all the difference
in the world.

我的手臂沒有長到足夠
擁抱我自己，
我還發現
在背脊上小小一處
交扣手指
就能讓整個世界
大大不同。

I promise you
I will try harder
to be better.
I
have battled with things
inside me
for longer than you know;
I do not know
what they are
or why they are there,
I only know
that they feel
managable,
defeatable,
when I
am around
You.

我答應妳

會更努力

成為更好的人。

我與內心

莫名的一切

纏鬥交戰

由來比妳所知更久；

我不知道

它們是何物

它們所為何來，

我只知道

我能

面對它們，

戰勝它們，

只要我在

妳

身邊。

I 我

Miss 思念

you 妳

so 至

much 深

讓疲憊的雙手與沉重的心靈平靜。
讓浮腫的雙眼與被竊走的呼吸平靜。
讓顫抖的皮膚與懷憂的嘆息平靜。
讓游移的目光與冷落的手指平靜。
平平靜靜。

You were the sound of wandering feet
and rainfall in the trees.
We thought,
god,we always thought
there would be enough
time.
I was the moss
that held the imprint of your shoe,
and I loved my indentions.

I was nothing,
but you found me.

You were everything
and I hold proud
the marks you made.

妳是林中徘徊的腳步聲和落雨聲。
我們以為，
老天，我們總以為
我們多的是
時間。
而我是苔蘚，
留住了妳的鞋印，
我愛這一身凹痕。

我如此渺小，
但妳卻遇上了我。

妳是一切，
妳留下的印記
讓我感到驕傲。

You
are the poem
I never knew
how to write
and this life
is the story
I have always
wanted
to tell.

妳
是一首詩
一首我不知
如何寫下的詩
而這一生
是一則故事
一則我老早
就想訴說的故事。

What if it's the there
and not the here
that I long for?
The wander
and not the wait,
the magic
in the lost feet
stumbling down
the faraway street
and the way the moon
never hangs
quite the same.

會不會我所渴求的
是彼處
而非此處？
我開始遊蕩
不再佇足等待，
迷途步履是
魔法
在遠方的街道上
栽了個跟頭
怎地月亮
高掛的姿態
也變了個樣。

And no matter the room
or the furniture between us,
I will brush your hair
back behind your ears
with my eyes
and I will kiss
the sides of your neck
with a glance.
I will unwind the fabric
and uncover the skin
and decorate it all
with goosebumps.
Then, I will blink,
find your eyes,
and realize I never
even left my chair
for a single
moment.

不論我們之間

房間或傢俱如何擺設，

我都會用我的眼神

將妳的頭髮細細梳到耳後

然後再用

輕快的目光親吻妳的頸側。

我要解開我的衣物

袒露皮膚

點綴上滿滿的雞皮疙瘩。

接著，我眨眨眼，

與妳四目交會，

然後才發現

我根本還沒有

從椅子上起身過。

I am so tired
of waking
to the blank canvas
of morning
and realizing
it won't be
painted
with you.

我受夠了
醒來面對
宛如空白畫布的
清晨
卻發現
妳不會
和我一起
作畫。

金屬冰涼，玻璃殘破；
木條老朽，碎屑如刺。
但且看，生意仍兀自盎然。
在破落與鏽蝕、頹圮與隙罅之間，生命萌發。
我們就是如此，一直都是，沒有什麼能阻擋我們
在礫石堆追著光明。看著我們成長吧。

a=3

It was when I
with fingers
like wands,
curled your lips
into a
smile,
that I hoped
you
realized that
I,
and only I
will be the
orchestrator
of the greatest
happiness
your life
will ever
know.

那時
我如魔杖般的
手指，
捲曲妳的雙唇
成一抹
微笑，
我只希望
妳
明白，
我，
只有我
能為妳
編就
這一生
妳所知的
最美好的
幸福。

CHAPTER II

PURE AIR AND THINGS THAT SPOIL IT

When 妳

you laugh 笑的時候

everything goes 所有 from 一切
hard 困難

to 都變成

the easiest thing in the world
世界上最容易的事

6

在這一生中，
有些時候你是軌道，通往神祕而
精彩的遠方。
有些時候你是火車，威武且滿載
著意志、動力、與達標的承諾。
有些時候，朋友們，你是錢幣，在
那些日子裡，全世界的重量碾壓
過你，而軌道只能兀自僵直而靜
默。你只要記得……很快地，會有
人跑向軌道。不管這一路通往哪
裡的天邊，忘卻火車從身旁駛過
的隆隆聲；他們會瘋狂地尋找你，
閃亮而光滑的你。他們會拾起你，
珍藏一輩子，當歲月逝去，留在他
們記憶裡的不會是火車或軌道；
而是你，錢幣。

Place your hands upon me
like a big tent preacher
and with a whisper
heal all that aches
inside.
Put your lips upon my forehead
and glance your eyes
to the sky,
tell me that I'll walk again
and tell me
I can fly.
Hold me like a revival
and shake the demons
from my skin,
touch me like a fever
and kiss me
like a sin.

像帳篷下的傳道者那樣
把妳的手放在我身上
用呢喃細語
療癒我
內心所有的創傷。
將妳的唇停在我的額頭
眼神掃向天空
然後告訴我，我能再次行走
告訴我
我能翱翔蒼穹。
擁抱我讓我重生
輕搖我讓我
擺脫邪祟，
撫摸我以狂熱，
親吻我以沉淪。

How quickly jealous
I become
of the wind
when it,
and not I,
gets the privilege
of properly
messing up
your hair.

我竟然
這麼快
就吃起風的醋，
誰教
搶下特權
理所當然地
撥亂妳秀髮的
竟是它
不是我。

I will love. More. So much love that no
one will have any idea what to do with me.
They will watch with a confused look and
wonder why I give so much and do not ask
for more in return. I will give it because
giving is getting and there is nothing
quite so important as emptying your heart
every single day and leaving nothing
undone, no declarations of it unsaid.

I will not only stop and smell the flowers,
I will plant them myself and watch them
grow old with me. I will pull over and
dance in every single rainfall, and I
will make snow angels even when there is
hardly any snow left for the wings.

I will never, ever believe in the words
"too late" because it is never too late
to be exactly who you wish, do exactly
what you should, say exactly what needs
to be heard, and live the exact life
you should be living.

我會去愛。更用力地愛。我的愛會多到所有人都拿我沒輒。他們會帶著困惑的表情看著我，猜想我憑什麼付出這麼多，卻不要求回報。我會付出，因為付出就是獲得，沒有什麼比每天放空心、盡該盡的責任、說該說的話來得更重要。

我不僅佇足嗅嗅腳邊的花兒，還要種下花兒，看著它們陪我成長。我會把車停在路旁，躍入雨中手舞足蹈。就算積雪少得可憐，我還是要躺在地上做我的雪天使。

我絕對不相信「太遲」的說詞，成為你想成為的人、做你應該做的事、說你該說的話、過你該過的生活，永遠不嫌太遲。

I would love to say
that you
make me
weak in the knees,
but
to be quite upfront
and completely
truthful,
you
make my body forget
it has knees
at all.

我很想說
妳
讓我
兩腿酥軟無力，
但
真要我
老老實實、
明明白白地說，
妳
讓我的身體
根本忘了
兩腿的存在。

跑吧。為你的人生、為你的喜悅、為你心靈的平靜與安寧。跑吧。你腿強身壯，你的肺渴望品嘗空氣。跑吧。中場步行的人生有什麼意義？

I 我

only ask 要的

for 只有

passion 熱情　　and 和

her 她的

tender 溫柔

狂喜

ecstasy

I want us. I want to swim in the
way you make me feel; I want it
to soak my clothes until they
become a skin, and I want that
skin to soak into my bones. I
want to become the way it feels
in the instant you stare at me
from across this crowded place.

我想要我們一起。我想泅泳在妳給我的感覺裡；
我要妳浸透我的衣衫直到成為我的皮膚，再滲
進我的骨子裡去。妳的目光穿越人群凝視著我，
就是那一刻，我想化身成那一刻的感覺。

If it's pieces of me
you find lying scattered
across the floor
under your feet,
please do not stare and wet them
with the regret-filled water
living in your eyes.
If cracks you find,
please, please,
tell me they are scratches
and never breaks,
handsome lines on weathered skin.
Don't ever tell me I'm broken
if you will not
be the glue,
and please
don't point out the fractures
if that's all
you're allowed to do.

如果妳發現
我已碎成了碎片
四散在地上
妳的腳下，
請不要凝望我，
不要用妳眼裡滿是悔恨的淚水沾濕我。
如果妳發現了裂縫，
請妳，請妳，
告訴我那不是破損
只是刮痕，
只是風霜在皮膚上留下的美麗線條。
絕對不要跟我說我已破碎，
如果妳不會是
那修補的膠；
也請妳
不要細數裂痕，
如果妳能做的
只有那麼少。

I pressed my ear to your chest
and heard the ocean beneath your skin;
tell me that the water's warm
and I will follow you back in.

Tell me you're a mermaid
and I'll walk into the sea;
I'll let the waves rise up
I'll let them bury me.

我把耳朵貼在妳的胸前
聽見妳皮膚下的那片海洋；
跟我說海水有多暖
我要和妳一同徜徉。

跟我說妳是美人魚
我會走進海裡；
我要興風作浪
要風浪將我埋葬。

You giggle,
softly,
and the sound of laughter
leaping
from your lungs
slows me to a crawl.
That laugh,
my god, that laugh
refills all that spilled
from me;
it is the
oxygen mask
to the plane crash
I have always
been.

妳咯咯地笑著，
如此輕柔，
從妳肺裡
躍出的
笑聲
放慢了我的腳步。
那笑，
老天，那笑
填滿了我散落的
空虛；
它是
氧氣罩
總在我
失事墜機之際
救我一命。

Was there always
this much night,
and didn't the moon
used to flirt
with me
from time to time?
How do I cross this
divide
and will I ever know
where you're hiding?
I am reaching
with fingers
stretched.

夜晚總是如此，
而月色不是該
時不時地
對我
賣弄風姿？
我要如何橫越這條
鴻溝
我又如何知道妳的
行蹤？
我伸出手
使勁張開我的
手指頭。

Part those sheets
like holy waters
and I
will worship your skin
like a born-again
believer.

分開床單
如聖水流淌
而我
我會敬拜妳的肌膚
就像重生的
信徒。

100

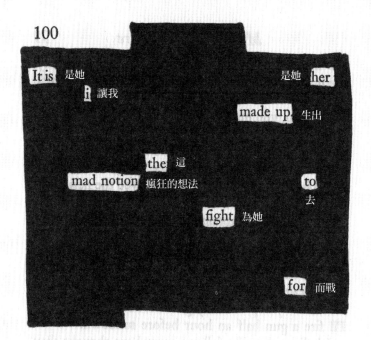

It is 是她　　　　　　　　是她 her

　　i 讓我

　　　　　　　made up 生出

　　　　　the 這

mad notion 瘋狂的想法　　　　　to 去

　　　　　fight 為她

　　　　　　　　　　for 而戰

I
am
too little
butter
on too much -
bread,
I
am
too many
thoughts
in too little
head.

我
是，
一小塊
奶油
然而麵包
太多，
我
有
太多的
想法
只是腦容量
不夠。

當黑夜逐漸變長、白晝逐漸變短，也許是我們相處的時間被延伸、被壓縮，請妳明白且記得：不論我們往哪裡去、不論我們做什麼，全世界都會看見我們留下的那道軌跡。我們燃燒的白熾火光會劃破藍空，所有人都將對我們做的記號嘖嘖稱奇。

Hold 讓

our 我們的

life 生活

Without any
無所

fear 畏懼。

92

I love you
with every
piece of me.
I will love
and love
and love
until I have nothing
left,
and then
I will make more
out of the nothing
that lives
where everything
once did.
I would
dismantle me
to put you
back together
again.

我愛妳
我的每一部份
都愛妳。
我會愛
一直愛
一直愛
直到我一無
所有，
然後
我會從空無中
生出更多的愛
因為萬物
原本就是
從空無而來。
我會
拆解自己
只為讓妳
再一次
完整。

```
I overheard the man
whisper,
"I am a lover
not a fighter,"
and to myself
I thought,
I
am in fact
both.
For is it love
at all
if it's not worth
fighting
for?
```

我無意聽見男子
低語，
「我是懂愛的人
而不是善戰的人，」
我心裡
暗自忖度，
我
事實上
兩者都是。
因為
若不值得
為之一戰
那還能稱得上
是愛嗎？

"Thank You"
she whispered soft
like it may
blow away
with anything stronger
than a breath,
"for fixing me."
"You,"
I sputtered out
like the first sound
of morning,
"were never
broken."

「謝謝妳」
她柔聲地說
彷彿任何比呼吸
更強的力道
就會把它吹散,
「修補了我。」
「妳,」
我急切地脫口而出
就像是清晨的
初音,
「從來不曾
破損過。」

暴雨將至，風勢漸強，陣陣狂風就要將你連根拔起。讓風來吧。讓它們肆虐，讓它們知道那一陣風摧折不了你；你會彎下腰。彎腰。儘管彎吧，因為你的堅韌超乎你的想像，因為你比破壞的力量來得更強大。

Come now the
flood
for you
have no idea
how long
I
can hold my breath.

洪水
正襲捲而來
因為妳
不知道
我
能夠屏息
多久。

Do you think it possible
that some people
are born to give
more love
than they will ever
get back
in return?

妳覺得可能嗎，
有些人
注定就是
要付出
更多的愛
比自己一生能得到的
回報更多？

或許是種意圖
PERHAPS AN INTENTION

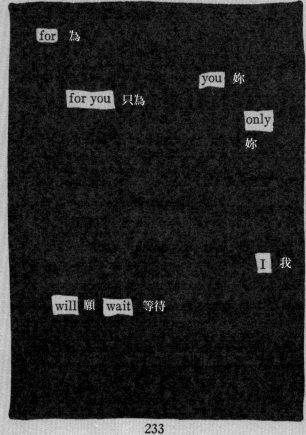

for 為

you 妳

for you 只為

only
妳

I 我

will 願 wait 等待

233

```
I promise to
   plant
kisses
   like seeds
  on your
     body,
so in time
        you
can grow to love
     yourself
       as
        I
   love you.
```

我答應妳
　會把吻
播在妳身上
　如種子
　種下，
　這樣
總有一天
　　妳
　會漸漸
　懂得
愛妳自己一如
　　我
　愛妳。

We
are the lonely remnants
of scattered dreams.
The phantom hands
rubbing forgotten backs
and the flashes
of eyes through the night.
Smiling or laughing
red with tears
hanging from the lids.
Too heavy to stay
too scared to jump.

We
are the missing pieces
of broken pictures.
There is not enough air
and I've not enough lungs
to hold the sigh
that relieves.
The absent fingers
tracing invisible lines
around swollen eyes
and stained cheeks.

We
are the staccato images
of lives not lived.
Swimming through our sleep
like broken slideshows
and skipping records.
The tired glances across
empty rooms
the shared breaths
through the choking silence.

We
are the stolen hope
of diverging paths.
The hair tangled in the hands
the slow closing
of soaked eyes
and the burying of our faces.
The distance between our bodies
as it grows wider.

我們是
夢境潰散後
孤單的殘存者。
看不見的手
摩挲著被遺忘的背
閃爍在眼裡的光芒
劃破黑夜。
微笑吧，或就笑到
脹紅了臉
眼瞼垂掛著淚水。
沉重讓我們無法停留
恐懼讓我們無法跳躍。

我們是
破損的圖畫
失落的殘片。
空氣太過稀薄
而我的肺也沒能
留住寬慰的
嘆息。
悠忽的手指
循著看不見的線條
撫過浮腫的雙眼
與染污的臉頰。

我們是
現在、而不是過去
斷斷續續的影像。
我們在睡夢中泅泳
如同播放著破損的幻燈片
與跳針的唱片。
我們是掃過房間的
疲憊眼神
是令人窒息的寂靜裡
共同的呼吸。

我們是
路徑分歧時
被盜走的希望。

Please
grab hold
of my neck
and whisper
sternly
into my ear
that you
did not forget
to remember
me.
You did not forget
the way I warm you up,
the pace
of our love.
The way my heart is tender
or how hard you laugh?
The way I smell
or how my arms
hold you
like they were made
out of the empty space
that surrounds
you?

請妳
緊抓住我的後頸
在我耳邊
堅定而輕聲地說
妳
不會忘了
要好好把我記住。
妳沒忘記
我溫暖妳的方式,
我們愛的
步伐。
我的心是如何溫柔
或妳的笑是如何燦爛?
我聞起來是什麼味道
或妳又如何
躺在我的懷抱
彷彿它們就是
圍繞著
妳的空間
做成的?

Right now
I smell
like old
books.
My hands
scented
with tired
words
and broken
ideas.
Right now
I smell
like paragraphs
and one too many
adjectives.

現在
我聞起來
就像陳舊的
書本。
我的雙手
沾滿了老掉牙的詞語
和零碎的
想法
散發的
氣味。
現在
我聞起來
就像使用了
過多形容詞的
段落。

If I am a wave
        then you
are the sea.
If you are a flower
        then I
am your bee.

若我是浪

那麼妳

就是海洋。

若妳是花朵

那麼我

就是妳的蜂。

我在此留步，獨自一人，期待草叢裡傳來妳的腳步聲。我在此等候，
安安靜靜地，就為一瞥妳的髮梢飛揚在風裡。我一直在此，倦了，卻
依然相信妳終將為我來尋。

Shall we sleep,
my love?
Fall into the hazy
palm of it
and feel its long fingers
wrap around our flesh?
Shall we take note
of the shallow indentations
its grip leaves behind
on our skin?
Shall we sleep,
my love?
Become the quiet sound
in our ears
of our heartbeat against the pillow?
Feel our breath
leave our lungs and imagine it
stirring together and dancing
above our heads?
Shall we sleep,
my love?
Trade all the light
and fury of this
for all the color and calm
of that?
Curl together and watch
as our legs become roots
that grow down from this bed
and plant themselves
into the earth below?
Intertwine.
Shall we sleep,
my love?

我們是否該睡了，
我的愛？
是否該墜入它若有似無的
掌中
讓它修長的手指
將我們的肉身包裹？
是否要留意
它的抓握
會在我們皮膚上
留下的淺淺的痕跡？
我們是否該睡了，
我的愛？
是否該成為我們耳裡
寂靜的聲音
成為枕頭上我們的心跳聲？
感受呼吸
離開我們的肺，再想像它
在我們的頭上迴旋、起舞？
我們是否該睡了，
我的愛？
是否要拿這兒的光明
與狂暴
去交換那兒的色彩
與平靜？
是否讓我們一同蜷起，
看著雙腿成根
從床邊向下不斷生長
好把自己種進土裡？
然後交纏。
我們是否該睡了，
我的愛？

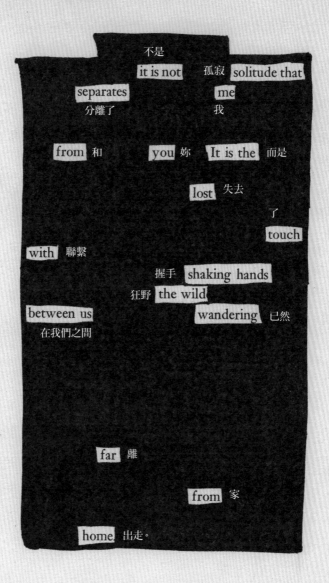

不是
it is not 孤寂 solitude that
separates
分離了　　　　me
我

from 和　　　you 妳　　It is the 而是

lost 失去

了

touch

with 聯繫

握手 shaking hands
狂野 the wild

between us　　　　wandering 已然
在我們之間

far 離

from 家

home. 出走。

真希望我知道如何耐住性子，就像它們一樣。真希望每一回我被推擠、壓迫、撞擊的時候，都能更堅持一點、更抬頭挺胸，去抵擋那些強大而難以對抗的無情力量。真希望我知道雲朵的滋味，降雨依舊使我氾濫。

If I chase
your echoes
down the hallways
long enough,
if I just
get ahold of them
once,
just once,
will it bring you
back
to me
again?

若我沿著
走廊
一路追尋
妳的回聲，
若我能
抓住它們
一回，
就一回，
它是否能帶妳
再次
回到
我身邊？

in 在

hope is 希望裡

strength 有力量

embrace it 擁抱它　and 並且　find 找到
me
我。

I, I have discovered, am an unsortable sort
of man. I open my mind to the pages before me
and the words fall out. They drip
like extra paint onto extra walls
or blood too rebellious to stay inside the confines
of racing veins.
I, I have discovered, am the sort of man that must write,
to keep locked tight the breath in his lungs.
Every word has a soul inside me, a body and a life
and don't they all deserve a chance at living it?
How can I stop now and leave widows of words
as those they found love with were destroyed by
and buried beneath the bombs of my apathy?
I, I have discovered, am the exact sort of man
that fixes, or tries, the broken around him. I pick up
the pieces, whatever those pieces may be and wherever they
have fallen from, and try to find the picture they once made.
I am the painstaking and careful tying of a popsicle stick
to the broken wing of a broken bird.
I am the breathless wonder, whether or not
she ever finds flight again.
I, I have discovered, am the sort of man who cannot help
but believe. In myself, in every single body else, in something
bigger than all of this, in hope and promise and the
unstylish and embarrassing dream that we can still be
exactly who we have always wanted to be.
I, I have discovered, am an unsortable sort of man.
If it is filing and sorting and finding order
in the orderless that suits you,
when you come upon me to file, I offer now
my most sincere apologies.

我，我發現，我是個不按牌理出牌的人。我對眼前的書頁敞開心，文字隨之傾洩而出。它們滴下，如同多餘的顏料落在外加的牆面上，或者像是叛逆的血液無法安於賽道般的血管裡。

我，我發現，我是個必須書寫的人，好把氣息緊緊鎖在自己的肺裡。每字都有我內心的靈魂、有軀體、有生命，難道它們不該有機會活下去嗎？在我以冷漠的炸彈摧毀、且埋葬了覓得真愛的文字之後，我如何能在此刻停手，拋下它們的寡婦？

我，我發現，我就是那種會修補、或試著去修補周遭一切破損的人。我會拾起殘片，不論它們是什麼、從哪裡落下來的；我會試著拼湊出它們原來的樣貌。我是如此孜孜矻矻、又仔仔細細地要將冰棒棍綁在折翼鳥兒受傷的翅膀上；我是如此急切地想要知道，牠究竟是否能再次找回飛翔的能力。

我，我發現，我是那種無可救藥堅持信念的人。相信自己，相信任何一個人，相信超越這一切所有的力量，相信希望與承諾與「我們仍然能做我們一直想做的自己」那個過時又尷尬的夢想。

我，我發現，我是個沒辦法被歸類的人。如果在混亂之中歸檔、分類、找出秩序是妳的作法，而妳非要將我分類時，容我致上最真誠的歉意。

```
I turn
(and
when I
turn the
whole world
stops
spinning)
to tell
(and
when I
open
my mouth
the words
fall out
like rain)
I
Love
(and
when I
say Love
I mean
more
than
anyone
has ever
loved
any thing)
You
(and
when I
say
You
the rain
stops
and I
mean
only
You)
        •
```

我回身

　（而當我回身時

全世界停止了轉動）

告訴妳

　（而當我啟齒時

話語墜落如雨）

我

愛

　（而當我說「愛」

意思是

比任何人

愛過

任何事還來得

更多的愛）

妳

　（而當我說「妳」

雨

即停歇

而我

所指無它

只有

「妳」）。

This kiss
and that kiss
on this piece
and that piece.
I am all
lips
and you
cannot help but
be
a perfect
pile of pieces.

這吻
那吻
落在這片
和那片上。
全部的我
化身為唇
而妳
便自然而然
堆成
完美的
一疊。

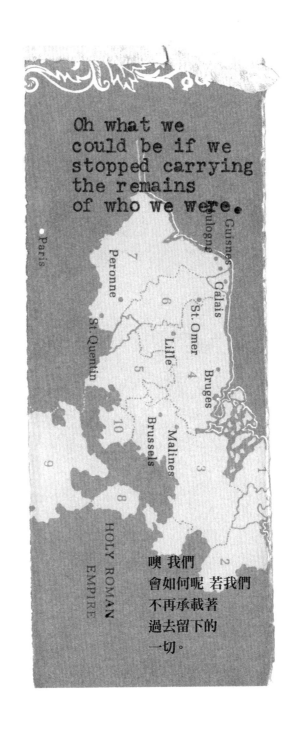

Oh what we
could be if we
stopped carrying
the remains
of who we were.

噢 我們
會如何呢 若我們
不再承載著
過去留下的
一切。

I might be lost at sea
but that will never mean
that I do not tilt my head
back, stare up at the stars
and sacrifice the salt in my
tears like an offering of my
most sincere and honest
gratitude for the way the water
never seems to stop rocking me
back to sleep.

我或許會在海上失了方向
但這絕不表示
我不會仰起頭，
凝望星空，
並且獻上我眼淚裡的鹽
作為祭品
以表達我最真心誠意的
感激，感謝這片汪洋
總是輕搖我入睡
未曾止息。

只要一點光，那就是我所需要的全部，
只要有妳給我的一點陽光，
我答應妳，一定會茁壯。

My ear stays pressed
against the ground
in all the places your feet
found rest.
I track the echo of you,
ghost steps on haunted floors,
and I wait forever
for the sound of footsteps
that might never walk back
to me again.

我的耳朵緊緊
貼著地面
不放過妳腳步停留的
每一處。
我跟蹤妳的回聲，
鬼步在魅影縈繞的地板上，
而我會永遠等待
這或許再也不會走回
我身邊的
腳步聲。

Dizzy
from the pace
of us,
did you hear me
whisper
"That
is how love
is made"?

我暈了
因為我們的
速度，
妳是否聽見我
低語
「愛就是
這麼做的」？

this constant tangle of

她的片段不斷　　　fragments of

　　　　　　　　糾結

　　　her 讓我　　　feel 覺得

　　　責無

indispensable To 旁

　　　　　　me 貸。

I am Midas.
I am Midas,
I should say,
in that all I touch
will wish and wish
that their skin
never bore the tattoo
of my fingerprint.
I am Midas.
I am Midas,
I should say,
except for I
can't even for a moment
before the ruin
see myself
in the gold.

我是邁達斯國王。
我是邁達斯國王，
我該如是說，
因為我所觸摸的一切
都會許下願望，祈求
他們的皮膚
不曾因我的指印
而留下紋身的圖騰。
我是邁達斯國王。
我是邁達斯國王，
我該如是說，
只是就算
在毀滅之前的時刻
我也無法看見自己
一身燦金。

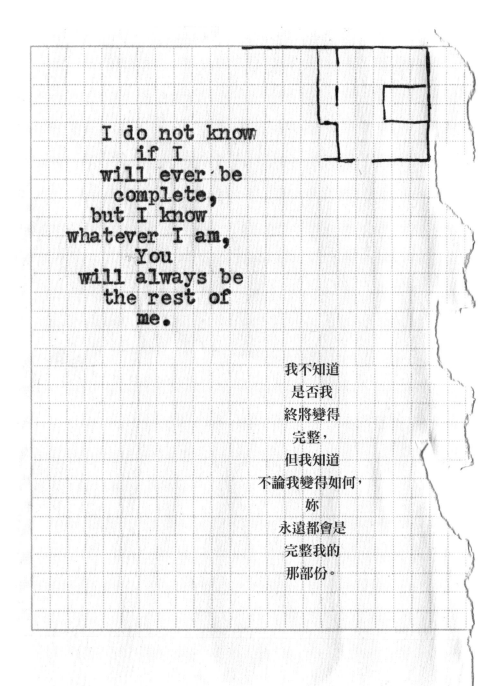

I do not know
if I
will ever be
complete,
but I know
whatever I am,
You
will always be
the rest of
me.

我不知道
是否我
終將變得
完整，
但我知道
不論我變得如何，
妳
永遠都會是
完整我的
那部份。

She juggles fire
every single day,
forces a smile,
and laughs
at the burns.
I will never stop
kissing the scars
that remain.

她每一天
都以火為戲，
她強顏歡笑，
對烈火的燒灼
嗤之以鼻。
我會親吻
她身上留下的傷疤
永不停息。

I 我

was in
惹 了

trouble
麻煩

for 因為

she 她

was a wild one,
是個野丫頭。

She walked past like it was nothing,
like she had walking feet
and I had staring eyes
and her scent followed behind.
It stayed when she left,
it found a way to stick to me.
She smelled like 5 a.m.
when it is far enough into the year
for light to play that early.
She smelled like rain that came
when the sun stayed out,
and for a moment it felt like
Mother Nature tripped
and spilled a bag of diamonds.
She smelled like home,
but the kind that is made
not bought, with memories
plastered like wall paper,
and still filled with the ghost
of whoever I was
before she walked past.

她若無其事地走過，
彷彿她有雙移動的腳
而我有對凝望的眼睛
她的芬芳如影隨形。
她離去後餘馥猶存，
縈繞在我身際。
她聞起來有清晨五點的氣味，
在時序已進入年中
光線大早便放肆嬉戲的季節。
她聞起來有烈日過後
雨的氣味，
一下子，它又像
大自然絆了一下
讓成袋的鑽石灑落一地。
她聞起來有家的氣味，
那是打造出來
不是買來的，以記憶
塗敷成壁紙，
仍然住著
在她走過之前的
我的幽靈。

An oceam
of
difference
exists between
making love
and
being made
by it.

差異
之
海
存在於
做愛
與
被愛所做
之間。

I
have blisters
on my
feet
from dancing
alone
with your
ghost.

我的
腳上
長出了
水泡
只因我
獨自
與妳的幽靈
跳舞。

祢是為了我而回來的嗎？

這是一切重新開始前的最後一道閃光嗎？

會有痛苦嗎？會的話又如何？我是不是夠仁慈？

我付出的愛是否比我內心所承載的來得更多？

我看見祢用光芒占據整個天空，我看見祢在雲間飛舞穿梭。

祢可以衝著我而來，但祢得先抓到我再說。

搞清楚……我會不停地奔跑

絕不罷休。

Through Golden Windows

We 我們

are 是

the 一首

poetry 詩

living 活在

in 我們

us 內在。

The black inside the color,
the dark hollow of your eyes
widens, slow, like an eclipse
to the light inside you.
If I were an ancient one,
I would fall to my knees
to worship the power
of the darkness you summon.
The breath, the soft rattle
that keeps you dancing
through your days,
abandons the ship of your lungs
and dives head first,
swimming on the skin
of my neck.
If I were a salt-stained sailor
I would jump to the sea
and smile calmly
as we sank together.

色彩裡的黑，
妳眼裡的陰暗空洞
愈來愈寬，緩緩地，彷彿要蝕掉
妳內在的光。
若我是古人，
我會雙膝跪下
膜拜妳召喚出來的
黑暗力量。
呼吸，讓妳
成天手舞足蹈的
柔軟手搖鈴，
拋棄妳的肺之船
並一頭躍下，
在我頸上的皮膚
游著。
若我是滿身鹽漬的水手
我會跳入海洋
並且在我們一同沉沒之時
平靜地微笑。

The shadow of my face
crawled slowly across
yours
as I leaned from side
to side
to kiss
your unkissed bits.
Maybe I
have always orbited
around you.

當我從這一側
到另一側
吻遍
妳沒有被吻到的每一處，
我的臉的影子
也慢慢地爬過
妳的臉。
或許我
總是在繞著妳
運行。

"What do you want for dinner?"
I voiced into the echoing part
of the kitchen,
and as the R syllable
bravely dove off my lips
I realized
that there would not be anyone
to catch him.

「晚餐想吃什麼？」
我對著廚房
發出回聲的地方說，
而當R的音節
勇敢地從我口中跳出時
我頓時了解
根本不會有人
來接住它。

```
I kiss you
    and
  on your lips
I taste the
    sea
  and the
    sea
has always been
   home
 to me.
```

我吻妳
並且
在妳的唇上
嚐到了海洋
而
海洋
一直都是
我的歸鄉。

I 我 remember 記得

us

我們 beautiful

美麗

and 又

exhaustless 充滿活力

we loved 我們愛

雙手

both hands

full of 滿是

life

我們

we loved 愛的生命。

129

A moment,
a smile;
a single burst
of laughter
that sounds exactly like
the rest
of my life.

一瞬，

是一朵微笑；

而一陣大笑

聽起來就像是

我的

餘生。

We stand shivering at the door,
terrified and panicked
that we have lost the key.
We waste lifetimes
in the waiting
because in the haze,
the painted fog
of our fear,
we forget
to check the handle
and discover
it has never been locked
at all.

-Tyler Knott Gregson-

我們站在門邊顫抖著，
害怕又驚慌
因為我們弄丟了鑰匙。
我們浪費生命
等待蹉跎
因為恐懼是
上了色的五里霧，
在朦朧之中，
我們忘了
檢查門把
我們會發現
這門根本從來不曾
鎖上。

—泰勒·諾特·葛瑞格森—

I might spill myself

我說不定會把自己給灑了

All 整
個 of

me 我

drain out 慢慢流失
leak. 滲漏。

be 要

擔心
afraid of
losing 失去 我。 me.

We are all
looking
for the right
reasons
to want to
get out of
bed
each and
every
bitter cold
morning.

我們全都在
找尋
正當的
理由
好說服自己
離開
被窩
在一個
又一個
冷得要命的
早晨。

Speak to me with morning voices
and glance across that pillow
with dawn in your eyes.
I want to hear you stir from sleep
and listen to the sheets
as they whisper of your rising.
What worth does this day hold,
if it does not begin
with you?

用清晨的嗓音和我說話，
從枕頭上望向我
用妳眼裡的曙光。
我想聽見妳在睡夢中的微動
聽見床單
在妳起身時窸窣碎語。
一天有什麼價值，
若這一切不是
從妳開始？

They look like letters,
they always have,
ink black and curled
with the rules
of alphabets.
They look like letters
but they are
and always have been
fingerprints
I left behind,
the fog on the glass
that remained
from where I stood
when I watched
you leave.

它們看起來像是字母，
一直都像，
墨黑而且捲曲
一如全套字母該有的
規矩。
它們看起來像是字母，
但它們是
一直都是
指印
是我留下的，
玻璃上的霧氣
未散
我佇立在這裡
目送妳
離去。

Flowers grew where you stood,
sprung from the soles of you,
strong despite the shade
from the shadow you left.
You leave gardens
every time
you walk away.

花兒在妳停佇的地方生長，
從妳的腳底萌發，
兀自強壯，儘管妳的影子
遮蔽了它。
每一回
妳離去
都留下滿園芳華。

we 我們　had 曾

a 瞥　　　glimpse into
見了

a perfect 一種完美的

life—
生活——

We wake 我們醒來　在吹　　過
to the　　sound
of wind through 樹梢的　trees 風聲中

Too much
me
too little
you.

太多的
我
太少的
妳。

Take it all away,
tear it and scatter yourself
into the breeze around me
and haunt me
with the pieces I cannot catch.
Hear me,
as you shred yourself
like confetti
that never found its
celebration,
hear me:
I
would love the scraps
of you.

全都拿走吧，
把它撕碎，把妳自己撒向我身邊的微風中
然後隨著那些我抓也抓不到的碎片縈繞著我。
聽我說，
在妳讓自己碎成五彩斑斕的派對紙屑
卻未曾覓得慶祝時刻之時
聽我說：
我
會愛著屬於妳的每一個小碎片。

噢我的靈魂，請你在寂然中找到安寧。
請你在天空中的黝黝樹影
雲朵下的灼灼山頭，找到
讓你語塞的平靜。聆聽
此刻，放慢你的心跳並聆聽，萬物
都會覺得來到你身邊的道路，萬物
都將安住，而匱乏的也會再次
盈滿。不要害怕，你已經
走過黑暗，而你仍然帶著
黑暗來臨前沾染的
色彩與餘光。

If only I could show you
the stuffing that stretches our seams,
the fluff that fills our empty bits,
and the space between our spaces.
If I could pull it all out
long and connected like magician's scarves
hidden in magician's sleeves,
I would show it to you with great fanfare
and with imaginary sweat dripping down
my forehead from the imaginary spotlight,
I would take one long deep and lasting bow,
for the truth would be spilled out in front of you.
Dangling from my hands, but the illusion,
the secret and the style behind the substance
would bring hands together in unison and in
uproarious applause.
All the threads that tied together made us up,
the spools born into us, unwinding, and the extra
we added along the way; carried, saved,
like we were bird beaks and our hearts, a nest.
When held out for you, arms length and decorated
with colored lights from the aging stage,
creaking floors and tattered seats,
here is what you would find, what we are made of
after all this time:

We are the memory keepers and the trappers of time;
stealers of stolen glances and breathless lungs
from all that have been taken away. We are the
noticers of subtle signs hidden in plain sight by a
benevolent universe bigger than we'd ever believe.
We are the thieves of buried fears and the confidence
left behind, left like jingling coins under sleeping
pillows after first teeth have been carried off.
We are the leapers and the builders of wings on the fall
towards the ground. We are the wingbeats and the sound
of flying. We are the directionless wanderers and the
destinationless travelers and we are the crumpled map
that never got packed to join us. We are the cinematic
lovers and the translucent curtains saturated in light.
The soundtrack to the moments without sounds and the
swiftness that two bodies can become one in the stillness
of a second. We, says the last string pulled out, the
final string that kept it all together, balled up tight,
filling us after all this time, **We, are the chasers
of the light.**

真希望我能讓妳看見是什麼撐住了我們的裂縫，是什麼補滿了我們的空缺，還有我們之間的空間。

如果我能把它全部拉出來，像藏在魔術師袖子裡的絲巾那樣綁在一起，我會盛大而隆重地表演給妳看，讓幻想的聚光燈照得我幻想的汗從額頭上不住滴落，我會向妳致上深長的一鞠躬，因為真相即將在妳面前展開。

這物在我手中晃蕩，但實相背後的幻象、祕密、與風格，會讓雙手齊聲而熱烈地鼓掌。

這些綑綁在一起的絲線組成了我們，與我們同生的線軸鬆開了，於是我們一路加進更多的線軸；這麼帶著、保護著，彷彿我們是一張張鳥喙，而我們的心，是巢。我伸長了手在妳面前展示，就是這樣的距離，再妝點上老舊舞台的七彩燈光、咯吱作響的地板、與破爛不堪的座椅，在這裡妳會發現，這些日子以來，我們是什麼組成的：

我們是記憶的守護者與設陷阱補捉時間的獵人；我們是小偷，所有被盜取的目光和屏息的肺都是我們下的手。我們是關注者，仔細留意著比我們過去所信仰更仁慈、更寬厚的宇宙，隱藏在凡胎肉眼所及當中的微小線索。我們是竊賊，偷走了被深埋的恐懼並且留下了自信，就像拿走第一顆掉牙後還留了幾枚銅板在枕頭下那樣。我們是跳躍者，也是在一路往地面墜落時打造翅膀的人。我們是振翅與飛翔的聲音。我們是沒有方向的流浪者和漫無目的的旅人，是從未被我們打包一同上路的那張破爛地圖。我們是電影的愛好者，是被光浸透的半透明帷幔。是無聲時刻的配音，是兩個人在一秒的靜默中可以合而為一的迅疾。我們——假設這是我們拉出的最後一條線好了，把所有一切綁在一起、緊緊地捲成一團、在這些日子以來讓我們變得盈滿的最後一條線——我們，是追逐光的人。

chasers
of the
light

追逐光的男人
和他的打字機

poems from
the typewriter series

國家圖書館出版品預行編目(CIP)資料

追逐光的男人和他的打字機/泰勒‧諾特‧葛
瑞格森 (Tyler Knott Gregson) 著；林育如譯.
-- 初版. -- 臺北市：商周出版：家庭傳媒城
邦分公司發行, 2018.10
　　面；　　公分　中英對照
譯自：Chasers of the light：poems from the
Typewriter series
ISBN 978-986-477-443-2(平裝)

　　　874.51　　　107005005

作　　　　者／泰勒‧諾特‧葛瑞格森 (Tyler Knott Gregson)
譯　　　　者／林育如
責 任 編 輯／賴曉玲
版　　　　權／黃淑敏、翁靜如
行 銷 業 務／闕睿甫、王瑜
總　編　　輯／徐藍萍
總　經　　理／彭之琬
發　行　　人／何飛鵬
法 律 顧 問／元禾法律事務所　王子文律師
出　　　　版／商周出版
　　　　　　　地址：台北市中山區104民生東路二段141號9樓
　　　　　　　電話：(02) 2500-7008　傳真：(02)2500-7759
　　　　　　　E-mail：bwp.service@cite.com.tw
發　　　　行／英屬蓋曼群島商家庭傳媒股份有限公司城邦分公司
　　　　　　　台北市中山區104民生東路二段141號2樓
　　　　　　　書虫客服務服務專線：02-2500-7718‧02-2500-7719
　　　　　　　24小時傳真服務：02-2500-1990‧02-2500-1991
　　　　　　　服務時間：週一至週五09:30-12:00‧13:30-17:00
　　　　　　　郵撥帳號：19863813　戶名：書虫股份有限公司
　　　　　　　讀者服務信箱：service@readingclub.com.tw
　　　　　　　城邦讀書花園：www.cite.com.tw
香港發行所／城邦 (香港) 出版集團有限公司
　　　　　　　香港灣仔駱克道193號東超商業中心1樓
　　　　　　　E-mail：hkcite@biznetvigator.com
　　　　　　　電話：(852) 25086231　傳真：(852) 25789337
馬新發行所／城邦(馬新)出版集團
　　　　　　　Cit　(M) Sdn. Bhd.
　　　　　　　41, Jalan Radin Anum, Bandar Baru Sri Petaling,
　　　　　　　57000 Kuala Lumpur, Malaysia
　　　　　　　電話：(603) 9057-8822　傳真：(603) 9057-6622
設　　　　計／張福海
印　　　　刷／卡樂彩色製版印刷有限公司
總　經　　銷／聯合發行股份有限公司
地　　　　址／新北市231新店區寶橋路235巷6弄6號2樓
　　　　　　　電話：(02) 2917-8022　傳真：(02) 2911-0053

■2018年10月02日初版　　Printed in Taiwan
定價／370元　　　　　　ISBN 978-986-477-443-2